Author: Johanna Hurmerinta. Designer and photographs: Johanna Hurmerinta. Editor: Tarryn Thomas. Publisher: Johanna Hurmerinta. Distributor: IngramSpark. ISBN hardcopy: 978-952-94-4702-2

INTRODUCTION

Hi. My name is Johanna. I love underwater photography. I also love writing stories and reading books.

I wrote this children's book so that you can enjoy beautiful photography of our underwater world, as well as a fun and exciting story about the Picassofish and his adventures.

With this book I hope to inspire children all over the world to learn about the beauty and significance of the oceans and their sealife.

This story book also tells its readers about the importance of friendship, helping others and being curious. These are all key things in life.

THE RED SEA

The Red Sea is the result of the slow separation of the African and Arabian tectonic plates. The coastal region is between 1-1600 feet deep.

The Red Sea is warmer than other seas, due to it being a closed body of water. The temperature of the water is above 68 °F during the winter. During the summer months, the water close to the coral reefs can be as warm as 95 °F.

The Red Sea is 35% saltier than most other seas, which gives it unique health benefits.

It is so exciting to dive into the Red Sea. The minute you go underwater, you are surrounded by silence and beauty. There are hundreds of colorful and attractive fish and corals in the sea!

PETE THE PICASSOFISH

Hi! My name is Pete the Picassofish. I live in a beautiful and colorful coral reef in the Red Sea. They say I look a bit funny. Some say I remind them of the art of a painter named Picasso. Well, I just think it's fun to be a little bit different than all the others! That means I am special.

My head is a bit bigger than others', and some teased me about it before. But then my great friend Paul the Parrotfish helped me, and told the bullies that it is not okay to mock anyone. The most important thing in life is to be nice to everyone. After that day no one has teased me anymore.

I love to be with my friends. We swim around the reef. Sometimes we play hide-and-seek. And sometimes we swim a bit further than before, just to see if there might be something exciting to find!

Let me tell you about my friends and my exciting life.

PETE AND HIS SMALL FRIENDS

Willy the Whitebelly Damsel has a white belly, just as his name says. Willy is a small fish, only five inches long. Willy likes to hide in the corals.

He doesn't like to be disturbed all the time, and that is okay. Some like to be alone and some like to have friends around all the time.

Willy has a secret: he can tell funny jokes. But not everyone knows this, as he tells the jokes only to his best friends. I like the one about Willy farting and making bubbles in the water. Willy likes to hide behind big corals and make bubbles. That scares some fish, as they think some divers are close and might try to catch some fish for the home aquariums. Then Willy stops farting and peeks through the small holes in the corals.

He does not mean to frighten the other fish too much, he just thinks it is fun to see the fish react so quickly and hide.

Sally the Sulphur Damsel is a lovely yellow fish. She likes the areas of the reef that have a lot of corals. She is fascinated about the beauty of the colorful corals.

Sally is very curious: you never know where she is swimming, and what she might find. I remember the day when Sally whistled for help. I swam as fast as I could to find her. She was stuck in a small cave inside the corals!

I had to swim around the large corals many times before I found a bigger opening, so she could get out.

She learnt that it is great to be curious, but it is also important to make smart decisions and stay safe! She will not swim into all small caves after this.

Jay the Jewelfish is so beautiful. I like Jay's coloring. It looks as though she is covered with small jewels. She sparkles in the sunlight. It is Jay's birthday today! I shall congratulate her. I do not have a present for her, but maybe that's okay.

"Hey, Jay, happy birthday to you! How will you celebrate today? I do not have a present for you yet, but I will try to find something later."

"Hello Pete. Thank you for remembering my birthday. That means a lot to me. I thought I would ask you if you would like to spend some time with me and swim to the other side of the reef to find something new to eat. Will you come with me? It is fun to swim together. You don't need to get a present for me! Your friendship is the best gift on my birthday," Jay says. We swim for fifteen minutes and find a new place. We do not find anything new to eat, but we have a lot of fun looking at the exciting corals.

The Sergeant Major, who we call Pintano, likes to come and have a chat every day with me. He is so curious about everything. He is also such a storyteller!

I remember one of his stories very well. It was a warm evening in August, when Pintano decided to swim all the way to the end of the coral reef, where the deep sea starts. It was a magical moment for him, to stare at the depths of the sea and enjoy the last rays from the sun in the sky above.

Suddenly he saw something come closer. Something quite big. He could not move. His heart raced and he thought he should swim quickly to safety. Then a big fish swam closer and Pintano almost fainted.

It was the scary and moody Barry Barracuda!

Pintano had never been so afraid in his life. Suddenly Barry stopped swimming and just stared at Pintano. Then Barry frowned and swam away. He likes to do this to small fish.

Pintano was so relieved that he swam quickly home and stayed there until the next morning.

The Crown Butterflyfish, Clara and Cole, are always so friendly and cheerful.

Clara and Cole like to swim together. They are not as social as some of my other friends, but they come and say hello to me a few times per week.

Clara and Cole are so much fun! Today we'll go to explore a magical place that they've found. They say it's best to go there early in the morning, before everyone else is awake.

It's good that I put my alarm clock on, or I would not have woken up this early!

'Hi, there! How are you?'

'I am fine. It is a beautiful morning,' Clara says. 'Come, let's swim quickly to our new, magical place. You will love it!'

Cole shows us the way and I am so excited. What have they found?

'Oh my, this is gorgeous. I love the corals here.'

'And this is the only place where we can find gorgonians! They taste so good. There is something special about these gorgonians! Please don't tell anyone about this place, Pete,' Cole says.

I promise to keep their secret. That's what friends are for!

We spend one hour at the secret place. We are so happy and content with full bellies. This is the best breakfast I have had for a month!

PETE AND HIS BEAUTIFUL FRIENDS

Eve and Eddie are the Exquisite Butterflyfish. These two beauties swim all over the coral reef. They even look inside big and small caves.

I try to stay away from the caves, as you never know what might be lurking inside!

"Hello Eve and Eddie. Are you not afraid of what could be in the caves?"

"Yes, Pete, we are, but we look anyway. We are careful! If we see a shadow or something big moving, we swim away quickly," Eve says.

"I am not as brave as you. Once I was near a cave and a huge zebra moray almost got me! "

"Oh my, that must have been pretty scary. Well, we are so curious that we take our chances, but we are careful. Thanks for caring so much about us, you sure are a great friend," Eddie says, before he swims to check out another small cave.

I continue my journey among the corals. I think I will try to find Betty!

Betty the Bluecheek Butterflyfish is a joy to the eye. So bright and yellow, and so elegant. I like to go treasure hunting with Betty. She often finds the most magical places, and small treasures like delicious clams.

"Betty, hello. How are you today? Shall we go treasure hunting?"

"Sure thing, Pete. I love to go treasure hunting with you. Where do you want to go today,?" Betty replies.

"How about somewhere we have not been yet? You choose where, and I'll follow you!"

"Okay, Pete, come on, let's swim this way," Betty says.

We swim all the way to the far side of the reef. It is so beautiful here. So many different corals, and so many colors all around us. Betty always knows the best places.

"Come this way, Pete. I think I saw some fantastic clams over here," Betty yells.

We find many small clams and eat a few of them for lunch. They are so delicious.

"Betty, you are the best. I love these clams! What a great lunch."

Then Betty swims to find her friend Bobby. I decide to take a short nap after a busy morning.

PETE'S FUNNY FRIENDS

Some of my friends are quite funny. Some in the way they look, and some in the way they act.

Claudia the Clownfish is also known as the Anemonefish. It is because she lives in an anemone. She does not get hurt by the stings of the anemone, the way most of us do.

Claudia is funny and cute. She loves to swim close to her home, as she is a bit scared of the bigger fish. Sometimes other Clownfish visit her.

Once a week she is brave and swims with me, away from the anemone. She loves to sing. I love to listen to her when she sings. Her voice is amazing. I think singing makes her feel less scared.

A song each day makes life so much more fun!

Bobby the Boxfish is such a funny looking fish. He looks like a box! Sometimes we play hide-and-seek. I can never find him. He's so good at hiding in small caves. I shall go and try to find him now.

'Hi, Bobby! Wait for me. Shall we play hide-and-seek today?'

'Sure thing, but you won't find me. You never find me. Do you want to give it a shot?' Bobby asks.

'Yes! I close my eyes and count to ten.'

When I open my eyes, Bobby is gone. How can he hide so quickly? I shall go and have a look behind the pink raspberry corals. I bet he is there.

'Found you! First time ever.'
'I let you find me, so you would win this time,' Bobby said.

He is so nice! What a neat thing to do, to let me win one time.

Harry Hawkfish likes to lie on the corals and watch his surroundings. At the same time, he is looking for something to eat. He is a bit tricky.

He likes to be by himself. But sometimes he lets me come close.

Once he asked me to come with him to the far side of our coral reef. I like adventures, so we swam all the way to the end of the coral reef and looked down. The deep sea is magical!

Then we remembered that Barry Barracuda might be there!

We decided that it would be best to swim back home and not take such big risks, even though curiosity is good for the soul.

Jim the Jellyfish is glowing and glorious. But you'd better be a bit careful around him.

Jellyfish have tiny stinging cells in their tentacles, to stun or paralyze their prey before they eat them.

Inside Jim's bell-shaped body is an opening that is his mouth. I have heard that despite their name, jellyfish are not actually fish. They are invertebrates.

I love to watch Jim float in the water and glimmer in the sunlight. But I don't swim too close to him. Better safe than sorry, like my mom used to say.

Lucas the Lollyfish is certainly funny and unique. He likes to lie on the sand and on the top of small rocks. He hopes that something worth eating will come his way. He is a bit lazy.

He is almost black and looks like a sausage or dark cucumber.

I swim by Lucas every day and say 'Hi!'. Sometimes he replies. Sometimes he is taking a nap. I think he takes more naps per day than anyone else.

Lucas has a secret: as a defense against predators, he emits a toxic red fluid when his skin is touched. So, you'd better watch out and not touch him!

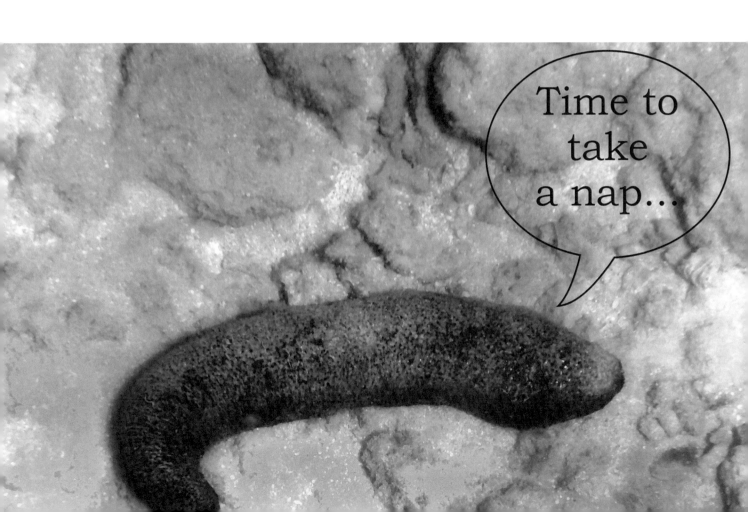

WHO IS THE FASTEST FISH?

I used to be a bit scared of Tim. He is the Orange-striped Triggerfish. Tim is very territorial! I saw him once swim right at Blake the Black Parrotfish.

I was worried about what was going to happen. Right before the two would have collided and gotten a big headache, Blake turned to the left. He decided it was not worth fighting with Tim.

Later I learnt Tim the Triggerfish just wants to have a little space of his own. That is something we have to respect.

Tim is also a great swimmer! He makes such quick moves up and down in just a few seconds.

Benjamin the Bluespine Unicornfish likes to swim around the coral reef. He is so fast. Sometimes I try to keep up with him, but he is too quick for me.

He says he is the fastest fish on this coral reef, but Tim just laughs about that. They compete often. We still do not know who is the fastest between them. I think Benjamin is. He usually wins when they have a contest.

I am not so competitive. But it is okay that some are. Some get a kick out of competitions. But it is good to remember good manners when competing.

Benjamin never gets upset if he loses a swimming contest. But Tim sometimes gets upset. I think he'll learn at an older age, that it is totally okay for someone else to win every now and then.

THE BEST YOU CAN DO IS TO HELP YOUR FRIENDS

Steve the Stingray is amazing. He helps everyone at anytime.

Last week I saw a lionfish get close to the Humbug family. The lionfish is a dangerous fish. In one minute, Steve was on site and got the lionfish to back off. Steve stayed with the Humbug family for hours. He wanted to make sure the lionfish would not come back.

Steve is loved by everyone. The best thing we can do is to help our friends and protect them.

Paul the Parrotfish is so nice to everyone.

He helped me when I was bullied at a younger age. He protects the small fish and is always caring. He is also very social. He likes to swim around and say 'Hi!' to all the neighbors.

It's great to have a friend like Paul. We all feel safer with him around.
We have agreed that I should whistle if I or some other fish are in danger. Paul will rush to help right away!

One time Uriah the Unicornfish tried to bully some smaller fish. I whistled. Paul came quickly to our rescue! Uriah decided to turn around and swim away.

DANGEROUS TIMES IN THE CORAL REEF

The coral reefs also conceal dangers. Some dangerous fish are sharks, barracudas, morays, lionfish, stonefish and scorpionfish.

We have no sharks close to this coral reef. I am so happy about that!

We have enough to worry about with Barry the Barracuda, the stonefish (which lie motionless and are often partially buried in the sand) and the morays.

I told you about Barry earlier. Let me now tell you about a few other dangerous fish.

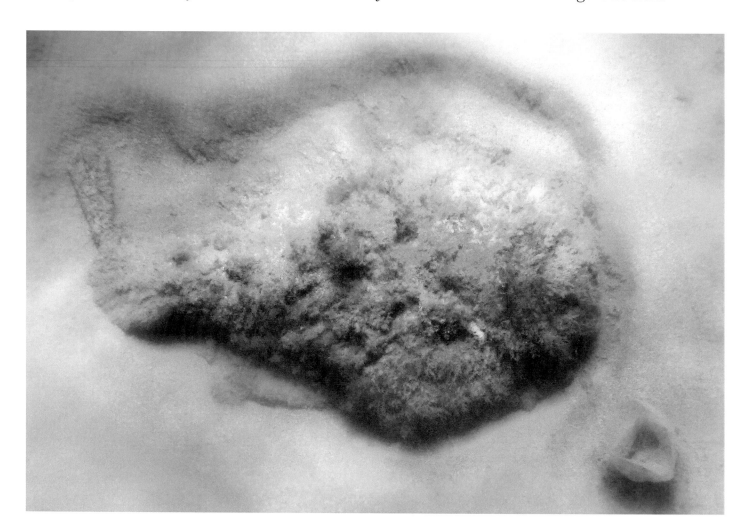

Gary the Giant Moray is a predator and is occasionally quite aggressive. Not so much during the day, but when the night begins, he comes out of his cave and searches for food.

I met Gary once during the day and the story goes like this:

I was minding my own business and swimming around a beautiful coral formation. I love to find new species of corals.

Suddenly a large shadow came over me. I got so scared that I could not breathe. I looked to the right and there was Gary! He is so big and scary-looking, I almost fainted! I closed my eyes and waited to be eaten. But nothing happened.
I opened my eyes and saw Gary swimming to another coral reef. I think I wet my pants.

Uriah the Unicornfish is so territorial and sometimes also a bit aggressive. When he is in a bad mood, I swim away quickly.

He has orange-colored, sharp, forward-hooked spines on his tail base. If he attacks, he uses the sharp spines and that hurts a lot.

He is also quite big, almost eighteen inches long. He is a vegetarian and loves to eat algae. As long as he is left alone, and can find the food he loves, all is well.

Though he is not very social, I like to watch him from a distance. He looks so elegant.

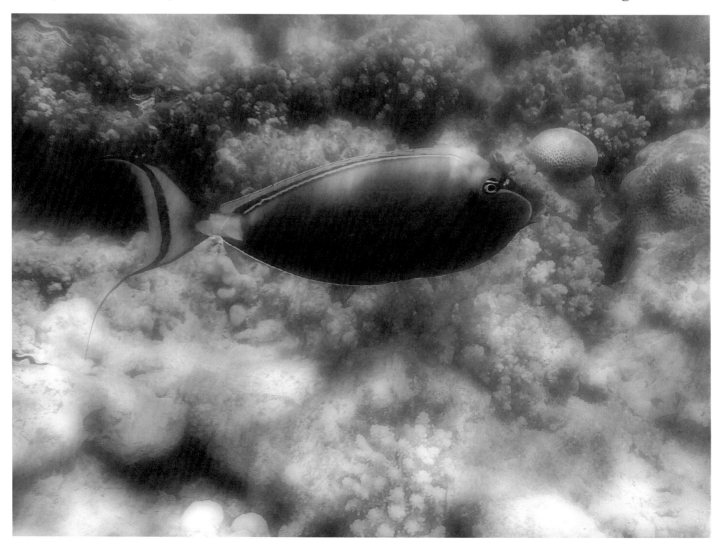

Zeke the Zebra Moray is smaller than the Giant Moray. But he too can get quite big, almost five feet long!

I sometimes see Zeke. But I avoid swimming too close to him. You never know what he might do. Zeke and his wife love to eat fresh fish, as well as clams, squids, scallops and shrimp.

Once I saw Zeke's wife lay eggs, and I was so surprised. She can lay up to ten thousand eggs at a time. That sure is a lot of eggs!

When she saw me, she got angry. I think she was scared. Maybe she thought I would steal and eat the eggs. I decided to swim quickly to another part of our coral reef.

HOW CAN WE HELP PETE AND HIS FRIENDS?

As the seas slowly warm and acidify with climate change, corals worldwide are bleaching. But in the Red Sea there is a ray of hope!

Scientists have discovered that a large range of corals in the Red Sea could be resistant to the climate crisis.

For some reason, many of the corals in the Red Sea are not affected by the rising sea temperatures. Scientists are studying the corals of the Red Sea. They try to find new ways to help other coral reefs around the world to survive the rising temperatures in the seas.

We can all help the health of the seas and our planet.

We should not throw plastic in the ocean.
We should not continue over-fishing.

ABOUT THE AUTHOR

Johanna Hurmerinta lives in Finland. She loves to photograph underwater. Johanna has dived in the Red Sea for 10 years. All the photos in this book are taken in the Red Sea.

THANK YOU

I would like to thank Tarryn Thomas for proofreading and editing.
Thank you to my husband for believing in my dream to create my first children's book.
Thank you to the editorial reviewers, who also gave me great tips:
Suzanne Wilkinson, PA, USA.
Alana Thrower, CO, USA.
A big thank you goes also to Jim Love, who supported my project from the very beginning.

I have found terrific information about Red Sea fish and corals in these books:
Collins: Coral Reef Guide Red Sea (Ewald Lieske, Robert F. Myers)
Global Press House: The Red Sea
Geographic & Co: Aqaba Underwater Paradise (Angelo Mojetta)

NEXT TIME...

This is my first story about the exciting adventures of the fish in the Red Sea.

In the next exciting and fun picture book you will meet Ann the Angelfish, Benjamin the Bluespine Unicornfish, Betty the Bluefin Damsel, Leon the Leopard Blenny, Lizzy the Lizardfish, Sarah the Sailfin Tang, Bruce the Broomtail Wrasse and some other funny and mysterious fish in the Red Sea.

CONTACT DETAILS

I would love to hear from you. What did you like most about this picture book.
You can write an email to me: johanna@hurmerinta.com

If you liked this picture book, I would be honored if you would like to write a short review on the webpage where you bought the book.

Welcome to my travel blog: https://travelwithjohanna.com
(my blog in English includes many fish photos and also small stories from the Red Sea)

If you are interested in seeing more coral reef, fish, and sea life photographies, you are warmly welcome to visit my photography gallery on https://johanna-hurmerinta.pixels.com

Lightning Source UK Ltd.
Milton Keynes UK
UKRC032152060223
416583UK00007B/297

* 9 7 8 9 5 2 9 4 4 7 0 2 2 *